Out and About

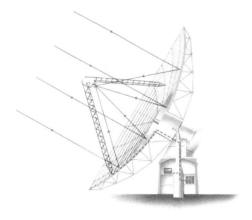

Text: Sharon Dalgleish

Consultant: Richard Wood, Curator, Powerhouse Museum, Sydney

This edition first published 2003 by
MASON CREST PUBLISHERS INC.
370 Reed Road
Broomall, PA 19008

© Weldon Owen Inc.
Conceived and produced by
Weldon Owen Pty Limited

Library of Congress Cataloging-in-Publication Data
on file at the Library of Congress
ISBN: 1-59084-178-6

Printed in Singapore.
1 2 3 4 5 6 7 8 9 06 05 04 03

CONTENTS

AT THE HOSPITAL

Doctors use ultrasound and X rays to examine and treat their patients. Machines use computers to show cross-sections of a patient's body and three-dimensional views of their organs. These machines can take a picture of the brain showing which parts are working while the patient is thinking, seeing, hearing, or moving.

hand-held probe

Ultrasound
This woman is having an ultrasound examination of her unborn baby to make sure it's healthy. The idea for ultrasound came from the sonar used by submarines.

In 1895 a ray was discovered that could pass through soft parts of the body and darken a film on the other side. Bones and teeth blocked the ray and left light areas on the film. Because the ray was such a mystery, it was called an X ray.

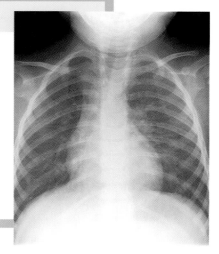

computer picture

How It Works
The probe sends special sound waves into the body. When they strike something, they are reflected and picked up again by the probe. A computer uses the reflections to make a picture.

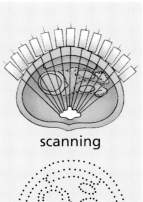

scanning

making an image

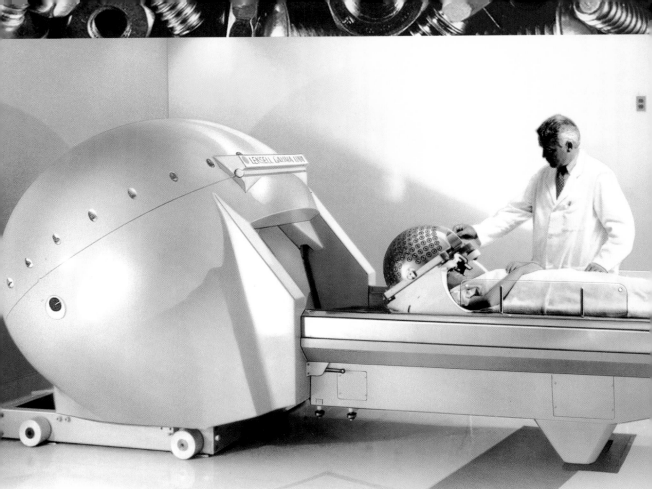

The Gamma Knife can't cut, but it can operate on a
brain tumor. Instead of a sharp blade it has about
200 radiation beams. Doctors use a special frame to
keep the patient's head still while they figure out
and mark where the problem is. They focus the
radiation beams through holes in a helmet that is
attached to the frame. The point where the beams
cross each other is the point that will be treated.

THE MICROSCOPE

The light microscope lets us see things that are so small we don't even know they are there. A magnifying lens bends the light rays from the object so that a larger image of the object is formed. The more curved the lens, the larger the image will be.

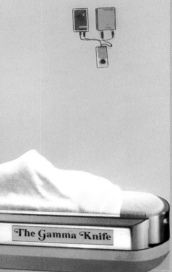

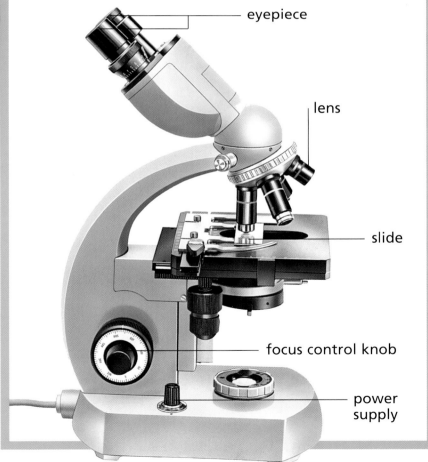

eyepiece

lens

slide

focus control knob

power supply

The Gamma Knife

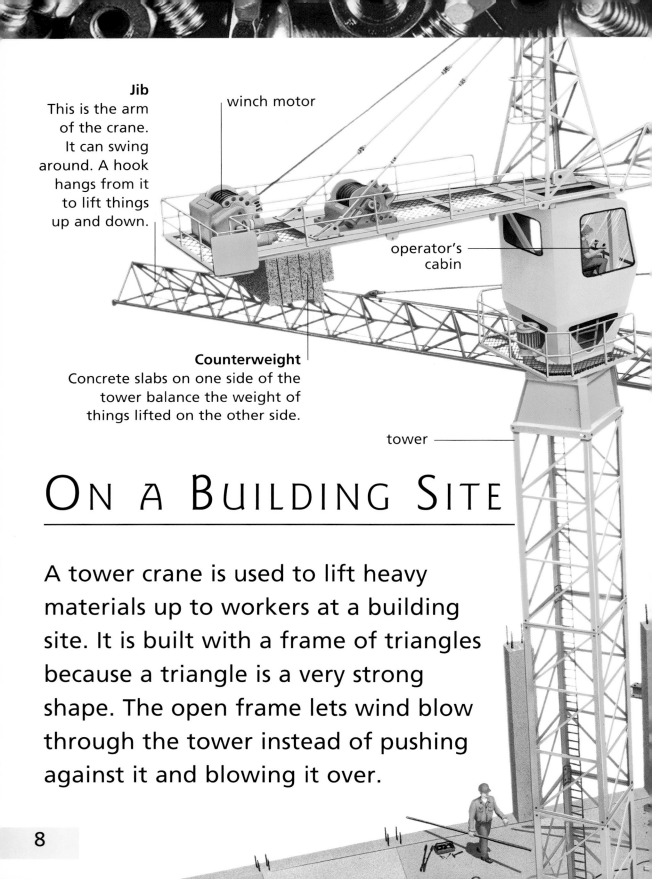

Jib
This is the arm of the crane. It can swing around. A hook hangs from it to lift things up and down.

winch motor

operator's cabin

Counterweight
Concrete slabs on one side of the tower balance the weight of things lifted on the other side.

tower

ON A BUILDING SITE

A tower crane is used to lift heavy materials up to workers at a building site. It is built with a frame of triangles because a triangle is a very strong shape. The open frame lets wind blow through the tower instead of pushing against it and blowing it over.

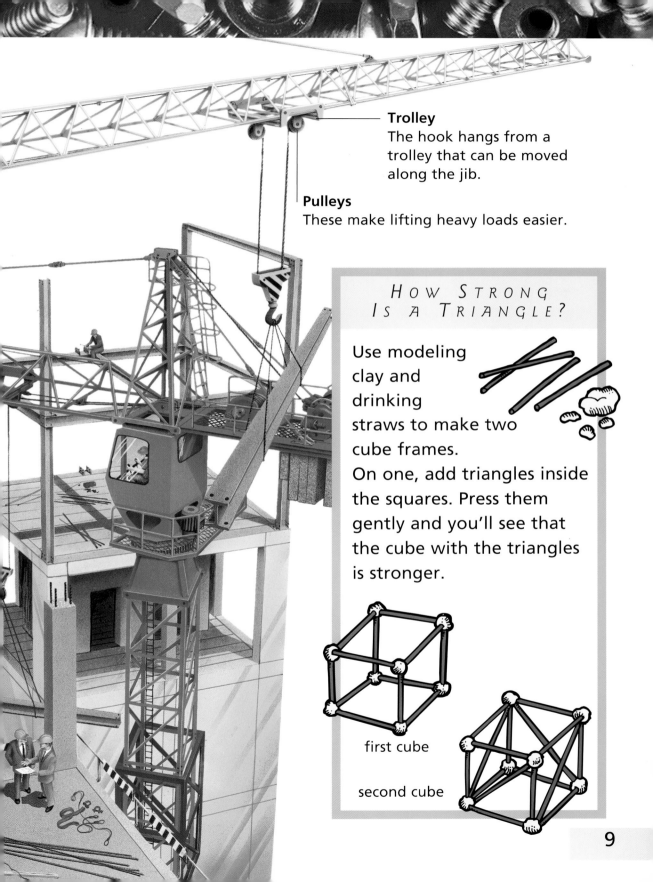

Trolley
The hook hangs from a
trolley that can be moved
along the jib.

Pulleys
These make lifting heavy loads easier.

HOW STRONG IS A TRIANGLE?

Use modeling
clay and
drinking
straws to make two
cube frames.
On one, add triangles inside
the squares. Press them
gently and you'll see that
the cube with the triangles
is stronger.

first cube

second cube

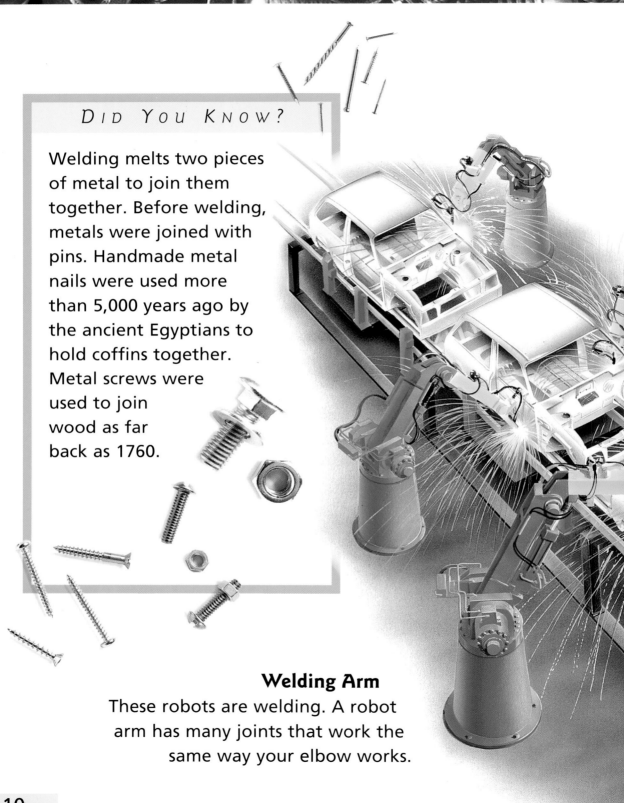

Welding melts two pieces of metal to join them together. Before welding, metals were joined with pins. Handmade metal nails were used more than 5,000 years ago by the ancient Egyptians to hold coffins together. Metal screws were used to join wood as far back as 1760.

Welding Arm

These robots are welding. A robot arm has many joints that work the same way your elbow works.

AT THE FACTORY

The first factories were dangerous and boring places to work. Today, robots are used for the worst jobs so that people work for fewer hours in safer conditions. In some car factories, robots use different tools to do nearly every job on the assembly line.

Computer-controlled Robot
These robots are controlled by a computer. Each robot does exactly the same work over and over.

Assembly Line
A conveyor belt brings the work to the robot.

GOING SHOPPING

Today, we use technology even when we go shopping. A laser scans the bar code and tells a computer in the cash register how much the item costs. Also, you don't need to go to a bank to get money. You can get it from an automated teller machine (ATM).

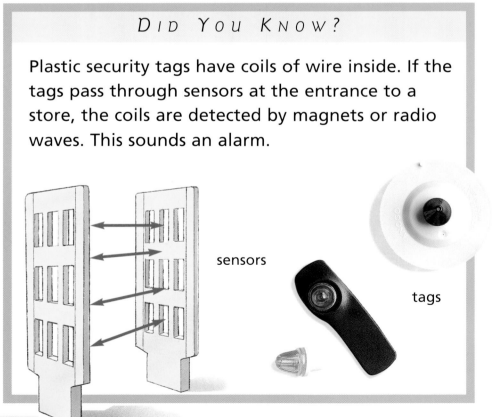

D I D   Y O U   K N O W ?

Plastic security tags have coils of wire inside. If the tags pass through sensors at the entrance to a store, the coils are detected by magnets or radio waves. This sounds an alarm.

sensors

tags

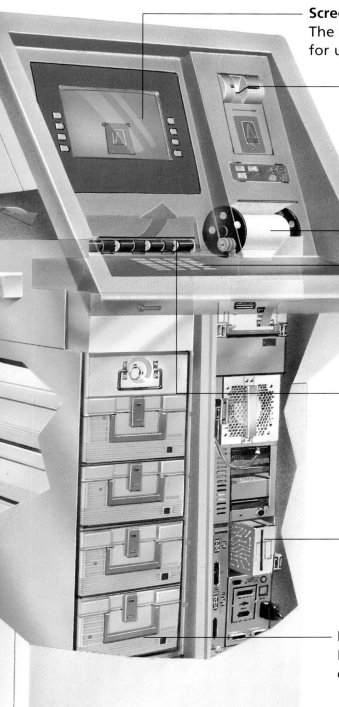

Screen
The screen shows instructions for using the machine.

Card Reader
This reads information recorded on the magnetic strip on the card.

Printer
A record of the amount withdrawn is printed on a receipt.

Keypad
The card owner presses keys to enter a personal identification number (PIN) into the machine.

Money Dispenser
Money is counted by the money dispenser and pushed out through rollers.

Computer Processor
A computer controls the machine and the messages on its screen.

Money Cassettes
Money is stored in boxes called cassettes.

AT THE AMUSEMENT PARK

A roller coaster ride feels exciting and dangerous—
even though you know you are safe. Cars hurtle
along tracks that twist and turn, dive suddenly,
and even turn you upside down. Today, most ride
frames are made of steel and don't need safety
supports. Cars and tracks are linked to computers
that make sure the ride is safe.

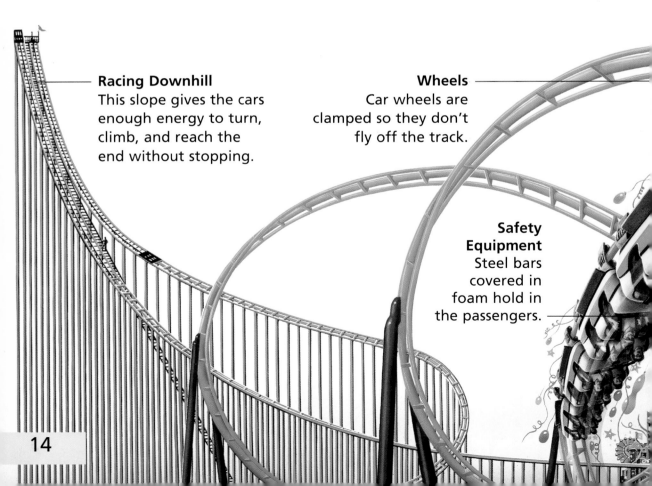

Racing Downhill
This slope gives the cars
enough energy to turn,
climb, and reach the
end without stopping.

Wheels
Car wheels are
clamped so they don't
fly off the track.

**Safety
Equipment**
Steel bars
covered in
foam hold in
the passengers.

Why Don't You Fall Out?

The curve of the track is designed so that passengers are pulled into their seats even when they are upside down. Here's how to prove it! Put a little water in a bucket. Swing the bucket around in a circle. The water will press against the inside of the bucket.

Step one

Step two

Feeling Funny
When the car dives suddenly, it takes a moment for your internal organs to catch up.

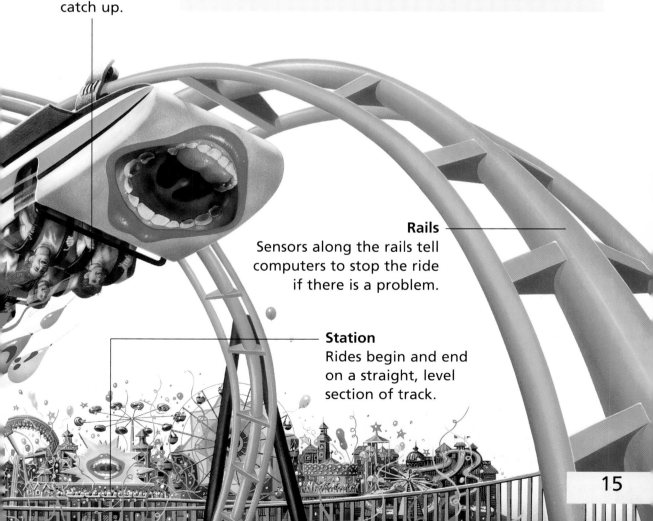

Rails
Sensors along the rails tell computers to stop the ride if there is a problem.

Station
Rides begin and end on a straight, level section of track.

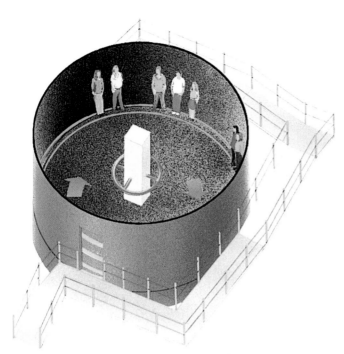

room starts to spin

This amusement park ride is a strange experience. Imagine standing against a wall. A motor begins to spin the room around. Suddenly the floor drops away—but you don't fall. You hang in mid-air! No, it's not magic. The spinning motion pushes you against the wall and holds you there firmly. This is called "centrifugal force."

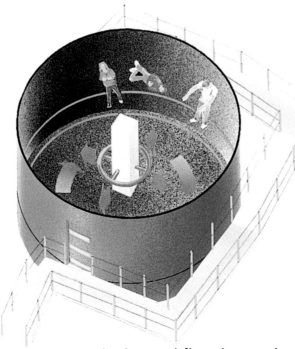

room spinning and floor lowered

D I D   Y O U   K N O W ?

Bumper cars are run by electricity. The current flows from an overhead mesh and down a pole at the back of the car to the motor. The motor drives the wheels.

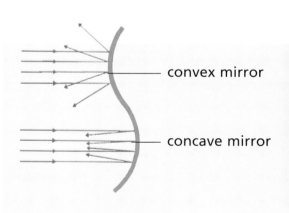

convex mirror

concave mirror

Is That Really You?

Some mirrors change the shape of reflections. A convex mirror curves outward. It makes you look shorter and fatter. A concave mirror curves inward. It makes you look taller and thinner.

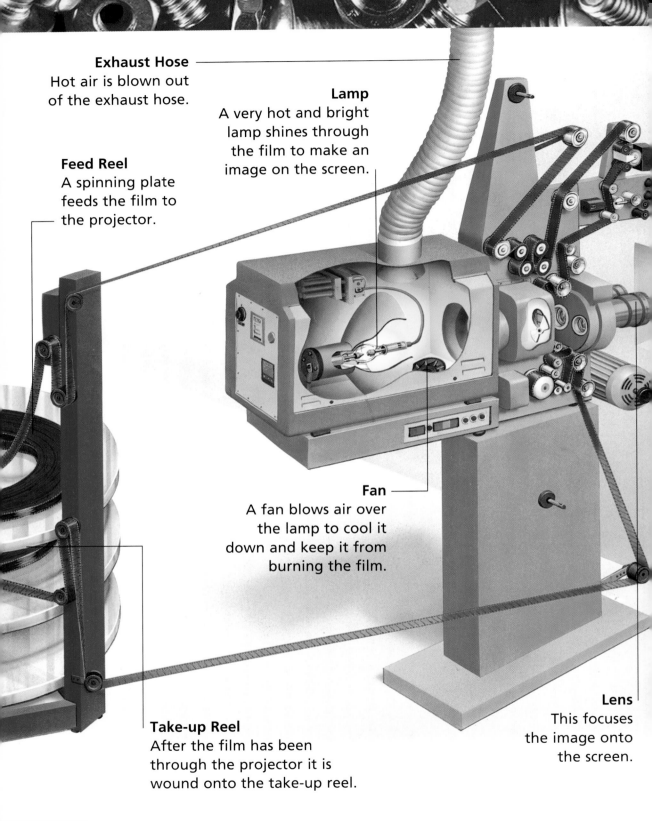

Exhaust Hose
Hot air is blown out of the exhaust hose.

Lamp
A very hot and bright lamp shines through the film to make an image on the screen.

Feed Reel
A spinning plate feeds the film to the projector.

Fan
A fan blows air over the lamp to cool it down and keep it from burning the film.

Take-up Reel
After the film has been through the projector it is wound onto the take-up reel.

Lens
This focuses the image onto the screen.

AT THE MOVIES

You have your popcorn. The lights go down. Get
ready—your eyes are about to be tricked! Film is a
series of still pictures that move quickly past
your eyes. Your eyes hold a picture for a
fraction of a second after it has moved on,
your brain joins the still pictures so they look
like one moving image. Each picture is called a
frame. A projector flashes 24 frames onto a
screen every second.

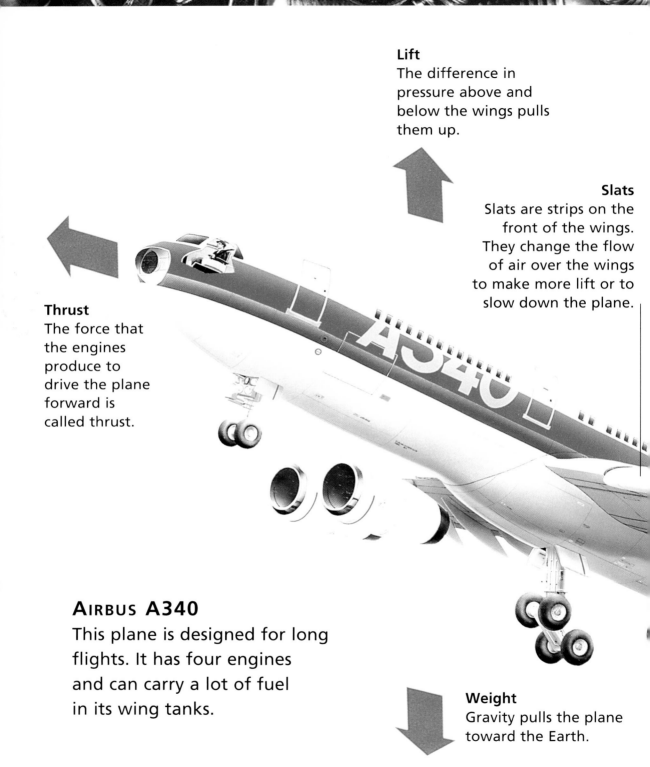

Lift
The difference in pressure above and below the wings pulls them up.

Slats
Slats are strips on the front of the wings. They change the flow of air over the wings to make more lift or to slow down the plane.

Thrust
The force that the engines produce to drive the plane forward is called thrust.

Airbus A340

This plane is designed for long flights. It has four engines and can carry a lot of fuel in its wing tanks.

Weight
Gravity pulls the plane toward the Earth.

PLANES AND AIRPORTS

Have you ever wondered how something as heavy as a plane can tip up its nose and soar into the sky? It can because of the shape of the wings! Air travels over the curved top of the wings faster than past the flat underside. This lowers the air pressure above the wings and pulls the wings up. This is called "lift."

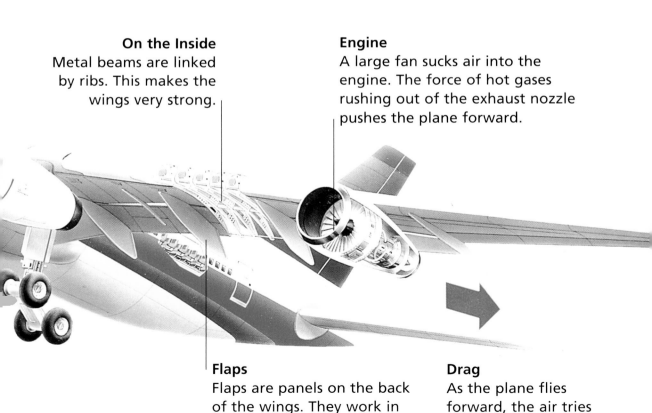

On the Inside
Metal beams are linked by ribs. This makes the wings very strong.

Engine
A large fan sucks air into the engine. The force of hot gases rushing out of the exhaust nozzle pushes the plane forward.

Flaps
Flaps are panels on the back of the wings. They work in the same way as the slats.

Drag
As the plane flies forward, the air tries to slow it down.

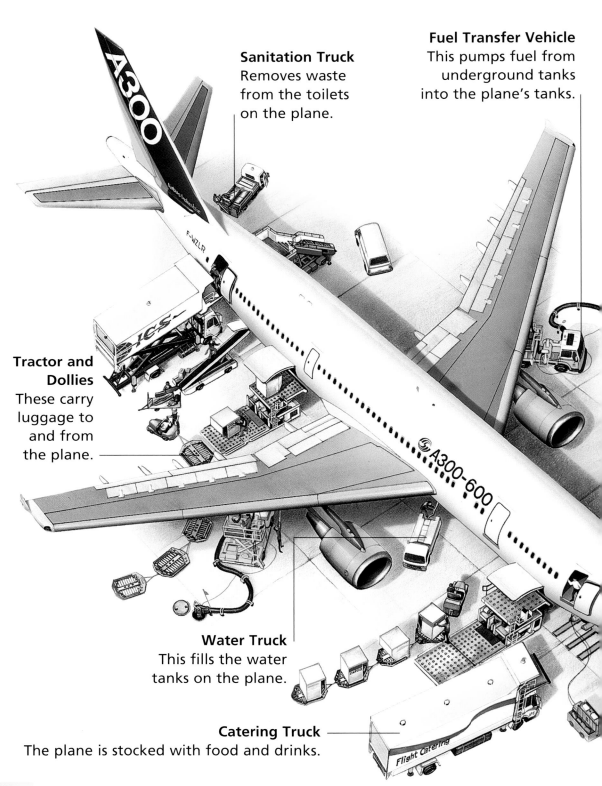

Sanitation Truck
Removes waste from the toilets on the plane.

Fuel Transfer Vehicle
This pumps fuel from underground tanks into the plane's tanks.

Tractor and Dollies
These carry luggage to and from the plane.

Water Truck
This fills the water tanks on the plane.

Catering Truck
The plane is stocked with food and drinks.

When a plane lands, the airport ground staff rushes into action. They unload it, clean it, stock it with more food and drinks, fill it with fuel, and get the new passengers on board. They also check to make sure that the plane's equipment is working so it can take off and fly again safely. All in just 90 minutes! The staff in the control tower watch over the airport and the sky around it. They tell the pilots when they can land and take off.

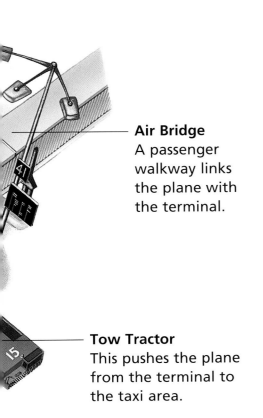

Air Bridge
A passenger walkway links the plane with the terminal.

Tow Tractor
This pushes the plane from the terminal to the taxi area.

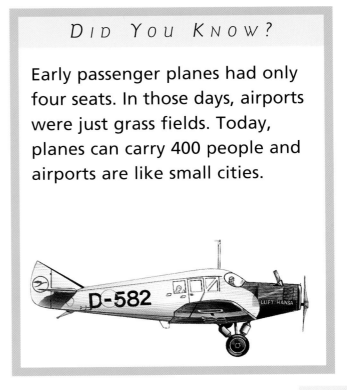

DID YOU KNOW?

Early passenger planes had only four seats. In those days, airports were just grass fields. Today, planes can carry 400 people and airports are like small cities.

Under Steam

A steamship is moved by propellers with blades that push against the water. These propellers are turned by huge steam engines that make a lot of smoke and noise.

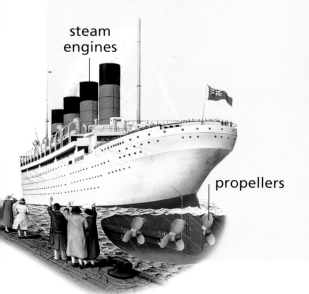

steam engines

propellers

Manipulator Arm
A robot arm picks up things from the sea bed.

PEOPLE MOVERS

Scientists explore the bottom of the sea in small submarines called submersibles. To make a submersible sink, the crew lets water into tanks to make it heavier. To make it come to the surface, the crew forces the water back out of the tanks.

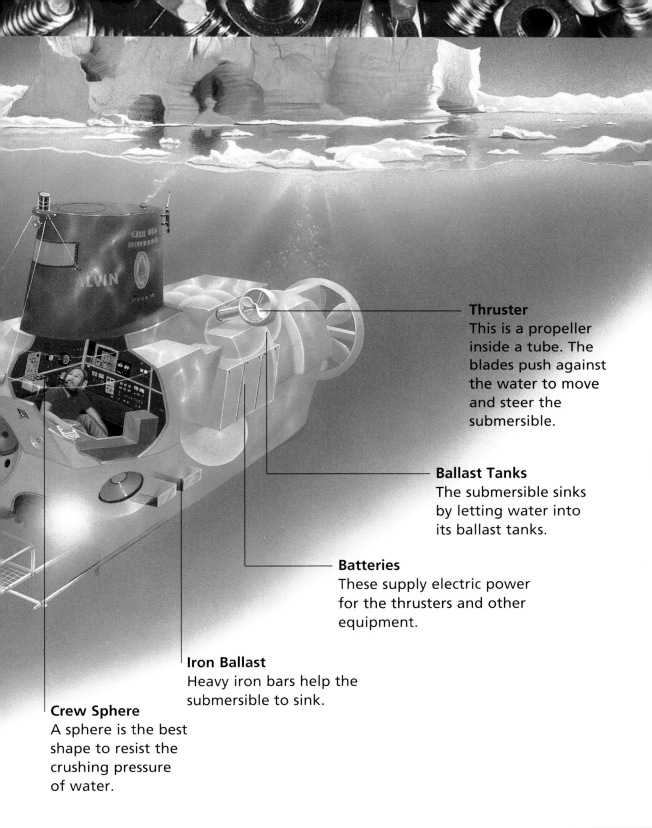

Thruster
This is a propeller inside a tube. The blades push against the water to move and steer the submersible.

Ballast Tanks
The submersible sinks by letting water into its ballast tanks.

Batteries
These supply electric power for the thrusters and other equipment.

Iron Ballast
Heavy iron bars help the submersible to sink.

Crew Sphere
A sphere is the best shape to resist the crushing pressure of water.

Magnetic Train

This train never touches its track. Magnetic fields make it float above. Magnets ahead of the train pull it forward and magnets behind the train push it forward.

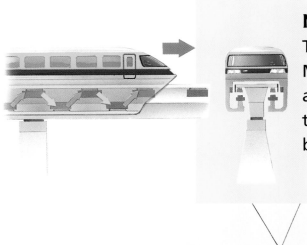

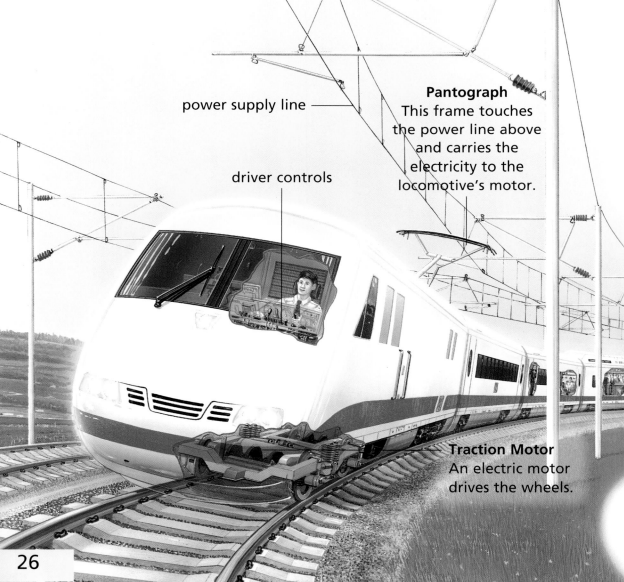

power supply line

Pantograph
This frame touches the power line above and carries the electricity to the locomotive's motor.

driver controls

Traction Motor
An electric motor drives the wheels.

The first trains were pulled by steam-powered engines. Today, some trains still use steam. Others use diesel engines, electric motors, and even magnets. Electric trains get their power supply from cables hanging above the tracks. These trains have smooth body lines so they can slip through the air easily.

MAKE YOUR OWN MAGNETIC TRAIN

1 On a piece of cardboard, draw the side view of a train. Leave an inch (3 cm) of blank cardboard at the base.

2 Cut out the top of the train and fold the base under. The train should stand up by itself.

3 Slide paper clips along the base.

4 Stand the train on a thin table. Hold a strong magnet under the table. Now move the magnet and see what happens!

What you need
- 1 piece of cardboard
- scissors
- crayons or pencils
- paper clips
- a strong magnet

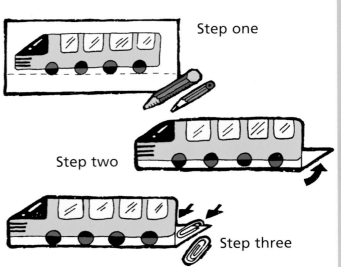

Step one

Step two

Step three

27

Radio Telescope

A radio telescope picks up radio signals from space. The signals bounce off a wide metal dish. They then come together at one point where they are picked up by an antenna.

Weather Satellite

This satellite has heat-sensitive cameras to monitor the temperature of the sea, the land, and the clouds.

OUT IN SPACE

Satellites are like mirrors in the sky. They circle the Earth to relay telephone calls and television programs around the world. Some have cameras and instruments to take pictures of the weather or help scientists gather information.

Low-flying Satellite
This satellite can dip down
to take close-up photographs.
It can see details as small as
2 inches (5 centimeters) across.

Communications Satellite
This satellite receives radio
signals beamed up to it
from Earth and sends
them back to a different
place on Earth.

GLOSSARY

antenna A device that receives or transmits radio waves.

assembly line An arrangement of workers and machines in which workers fit one part to a product as it moves past them on a conveyor belt.

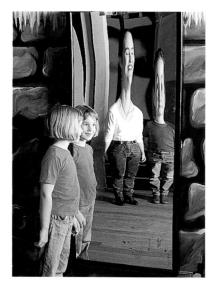

cross-section A drawing of something that shows what you would see if you could cut it through the middle.

gravity The force that pulls us down to the ground and keeps the Earth circling the Sun.

radio waves Invisible electromagnetic waves that carry information, such as the human voice.

sonar A device that sends sound through water and then detects echoes as they bounce off objects. It stands for "sound navigation and ranging."

ultrasound A high-pitched sound that humans cannot hear.

INDEX

PICTURE AND ILLUSTRATION CREDITS

BOOKS IN THIS SERIES